Clarke's ↑

me ↗

# Tell Me Again
## About the Night I Was Born
by Jamie Lee Curtis
illustrated by Laura Cornell

Joanna Cotler Books

*An Imprint of* HarperCollins*Publishers*

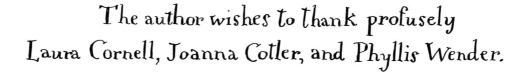

The author wishes to thank profusely
Laura Cornell, Joanna Cotler, and Phyllis Wender.

Tell Me Again About the Night I Was Born   Text copyright © 1996 by Jamie Lee Curtis   Illustrations copyright © 1996 by Laura Cornell
Printed in the U.S.A. All rights reserved.   Library of Congress Cataloging-in-Publication Data   Curtis, Jamie Lee, date.
Tell me again about the night I was born / by Jamie Lee Curtis ; illustrated by Laura Cornell.
p.   cm.   "Joanna Cotler books."   Summary: A young girl asks her parents to tell her again the cherished family story about her birth and adoption.
ISBN 0-06-024528-X. – ISBN 0-06-024529-8 (lib. bdg.)   [1. Adoption–Fiction.  2. Babies–Fiction.]   I. Cornell, Laura, ill.  II. Title.
PZ7.C9418Te   1996   95-5412   [E]–dc20   CIP   AC   1  2  3  4  5  6  7  8  9  10   ❖  First Edition

For Annie, Tom and Chris
~J.L.C.

For Lilly
~L.C.

Tell me again about the night I was born.

Tell me again how you and Daddy were curled up like spoons and Daddy was snoring.

Tell me again how the phone rang in the middle of the night and they told you I was born.
Tell me again how you screamed.

Tell me again how you called Granny and Grandpa right away, but they didn't hear the phone because they sleep like logs.

Tell me again how you got on an airplane with my
baby bag and flew to get me and how there was
no movie, only peanuts.

MY

Grandpa Simon    Granny Jackie

Grandpa Washington    Grandma Lucy    Grandpa Henry    Grandma Miami

Dad    Birth Dad

Aunt Dinah    Uncle Teddy    Dad    Me    Uncle Jack    Mom    Aunt Clare

Clarke →    Me →

# Family Tree

Great Grandpa Fred

Great Grandma Donna

Great Uncle Earl

Grandpa Neal

Grandma Barbara

Great Aunt Mary

Great Aunt Martha

Birth Mom

Mom

Aunt Jenny

Uncle Steve

Cousin Tanner

Cousin Paige

Tell me again how you couldn't grow a baby in your tummy, so another woman who was too young to take care of me was growing me and she would be my birth mother, and you would adopt me and be my parents.

Tell me again how you held hands all the way to the hospital and when you got there you both got very quiet and felt very very small.

Tell me again about the first time you saw me through the nursery window and how you couldn't believe something so small could make you smile so big.

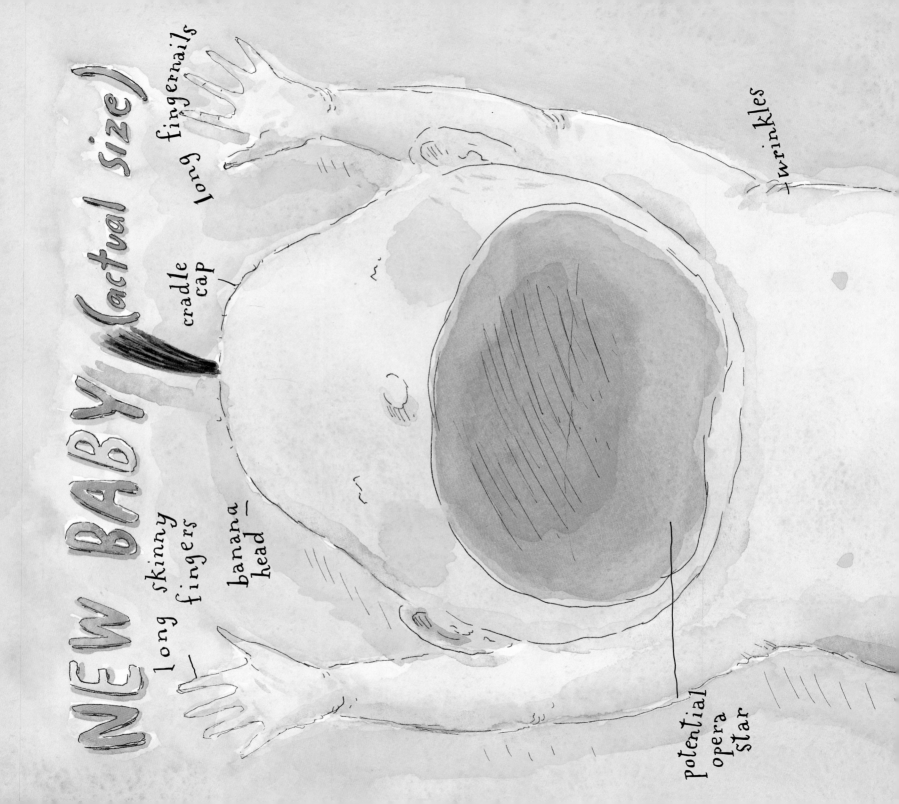

NEW BABY *(actual size)*

long fingernails

cradle
cap

banana
head

long skinny
fingers

Potential
opera
star

wrinkles

newborn
diapers

future
belly button

legs that rarely
straighten out

— Perfect
pink toes

Tell me again how tiny and perfect I was.

Tell me again about the first time you held me
in your arms and called me your baby sweet.
Tell me again how you cried happy tears.

Tell me again how you carried me like a china doll all the way home and how you glared at anyone who sneezed.

Tell me again about my first bottle and how I liked it so much.

Tell me again about my first diaper change and how I didn't like it at all.

Tell me again about the first night you were my daddy and you told me about baseball being the perfect game, like your daddy told you.

Tell me again about the first night you were my mommy and you sang the lullaby your mommy sang to you.

Tell me again about our first night as a family.

Mommy, Daddy, tell me again about the night
I was born.

Dad →